ARE YOU A MONSTER?

GUILHERME KARSTEN

HeLLO!

I'm a brave and bad, really <u>BAD</u>, monster!

NOTHING AND NOBODY SCARES ME!

I'm on the lookout for a monster buddy to do **SCARY THINGS** with together!

HEY, YOU! YES, YOU! ARE YOU A MONSTER, TOO?

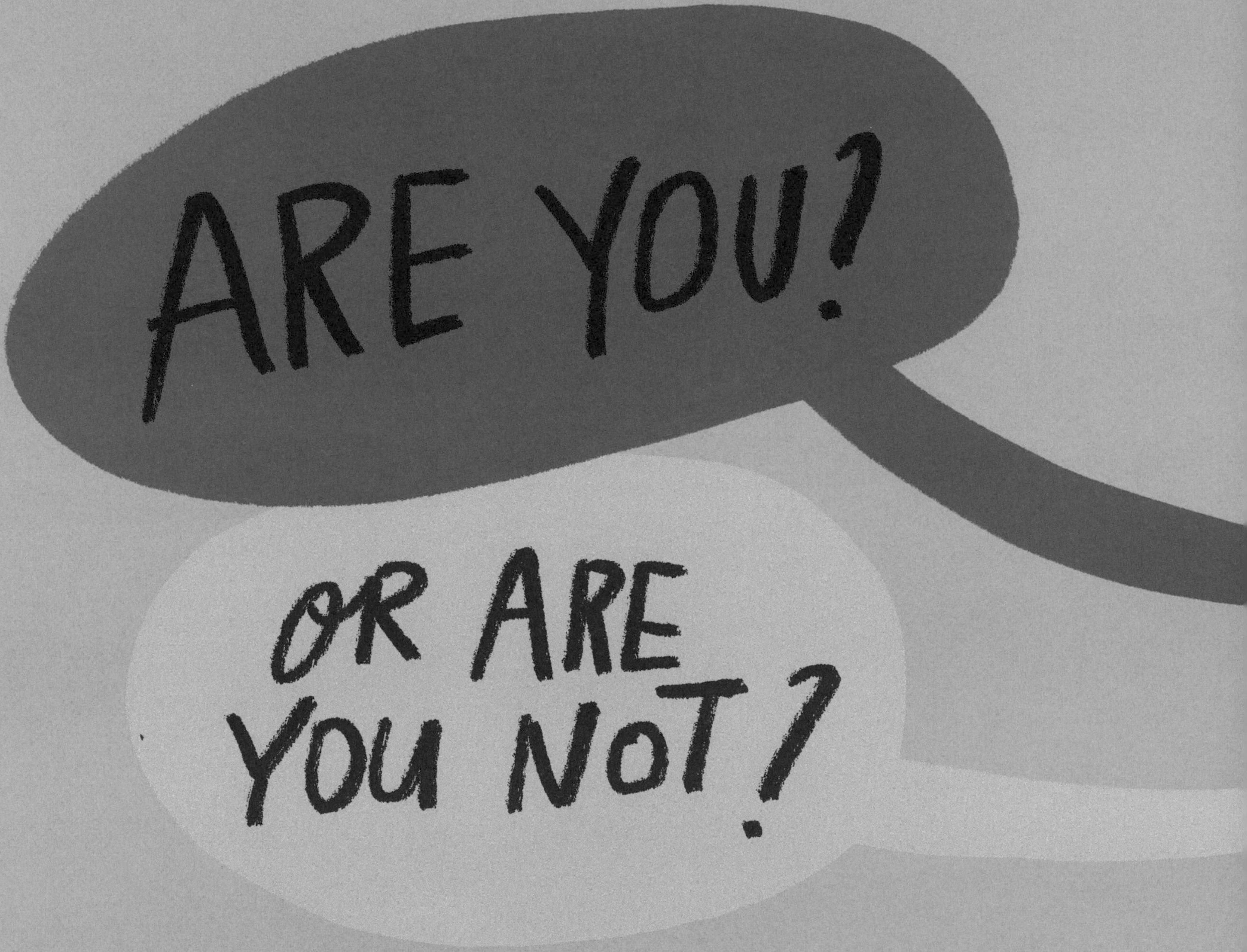
ARE YOU?
OR ARE YOU NOT?

OK, let's see.

Show me your LONG **and** POiNTY TAiL.

WHAT ?

NO TAiL ?

Do you have long, pointy nails?

Hmm... show me your

BIG...

OH, COME ON!

No yellow eyes?
No rough skin?
Not even spikes on your back?

OK, I'M DONE.

YOU ARE NOT
A MONSTER!

You can close this book now.

THE END

BYE-BYE.

THE END

What do you mean, you're upset? Why?
I'm looking for a monster and you are
not a MONS...

WAIT !

Show me your teeth again.

Can you make a **LOUD** noise?
Something like

GRRRRR...
or
ROARRRR?

Can you walk
like a monster?

STOMPING
HARD

on the floor?

Now, one last thing...
Can you do everything at the
SAME TIME?

GRRRR...

RAWRrr...

ROARRr...

!!!

THAT

Finally, I've found the most
SCARiEST,
REALLY BAD MONST...

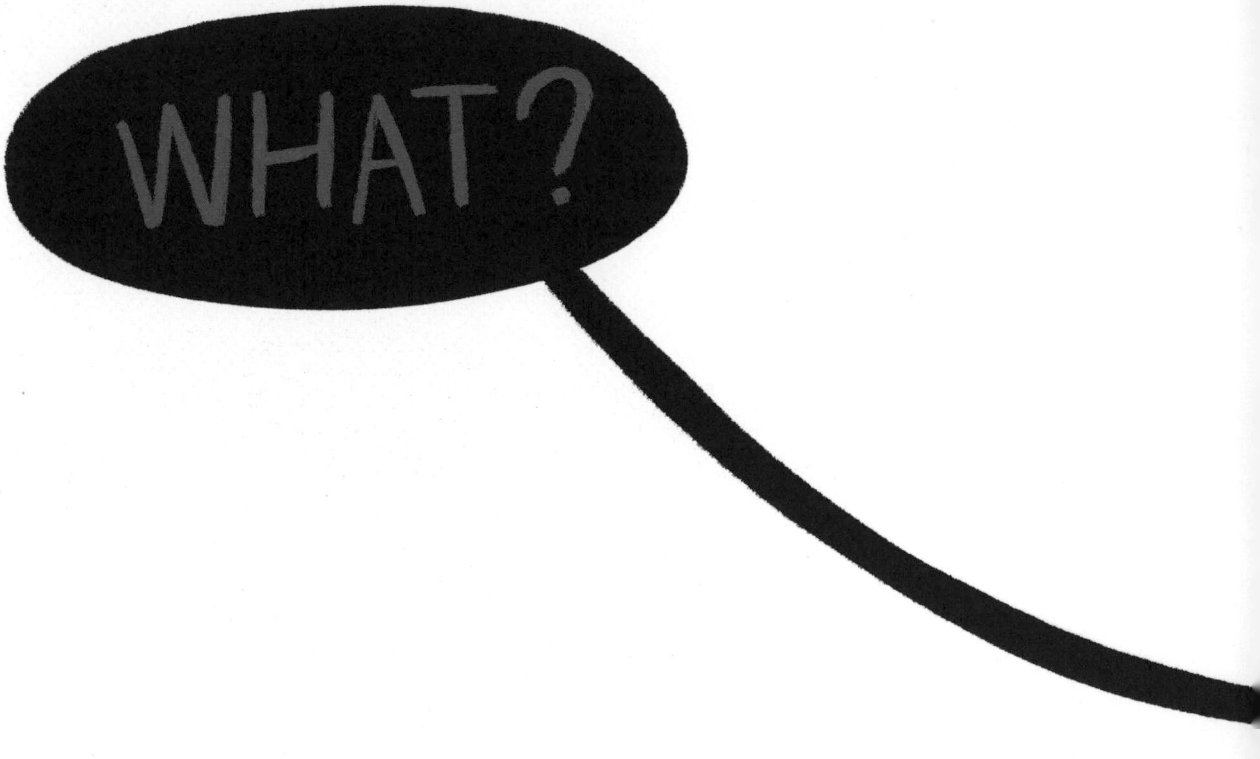
WHAT?

D-Did I just say S-S-S-CA-ARY?

Why are you s-s-st-aring at me like that?

We were just having a bit of fun, right?

OK, I'm not scared, but it really
is time to close this book, buddy...

I... I need to go home now.
My mum is calling me...

... I'm coming, Mummy!

... **Mummy?**

MYYYYY!!!

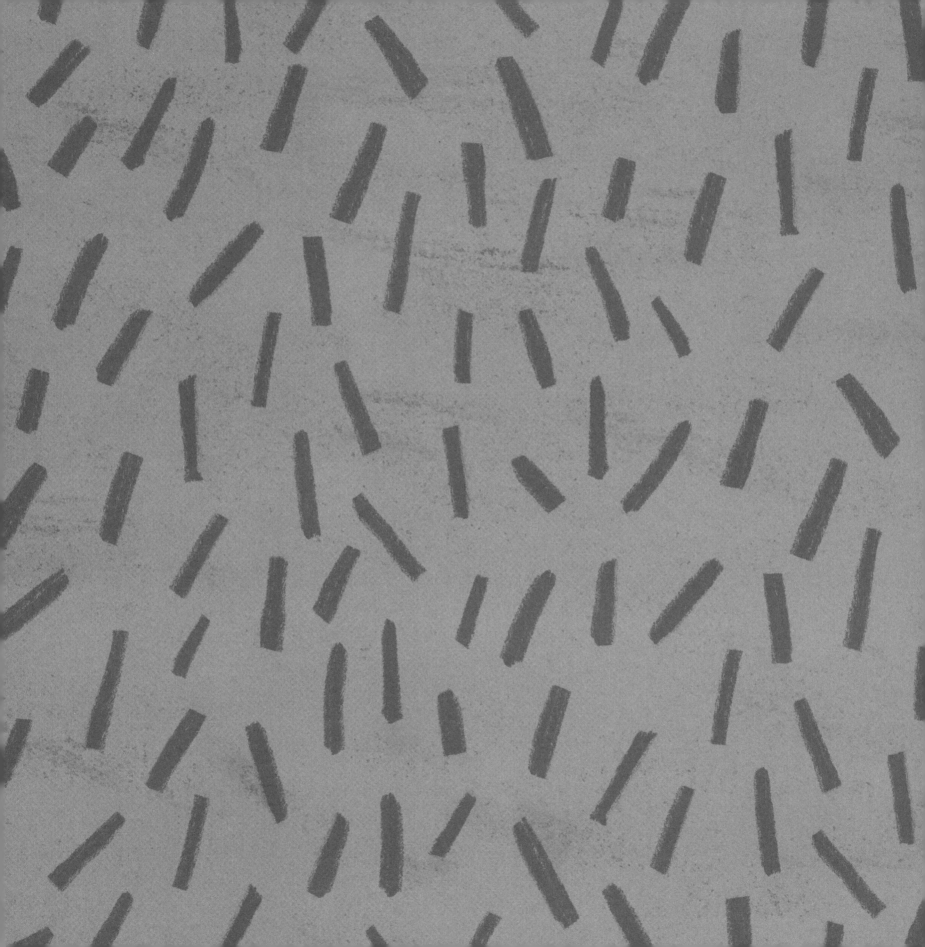